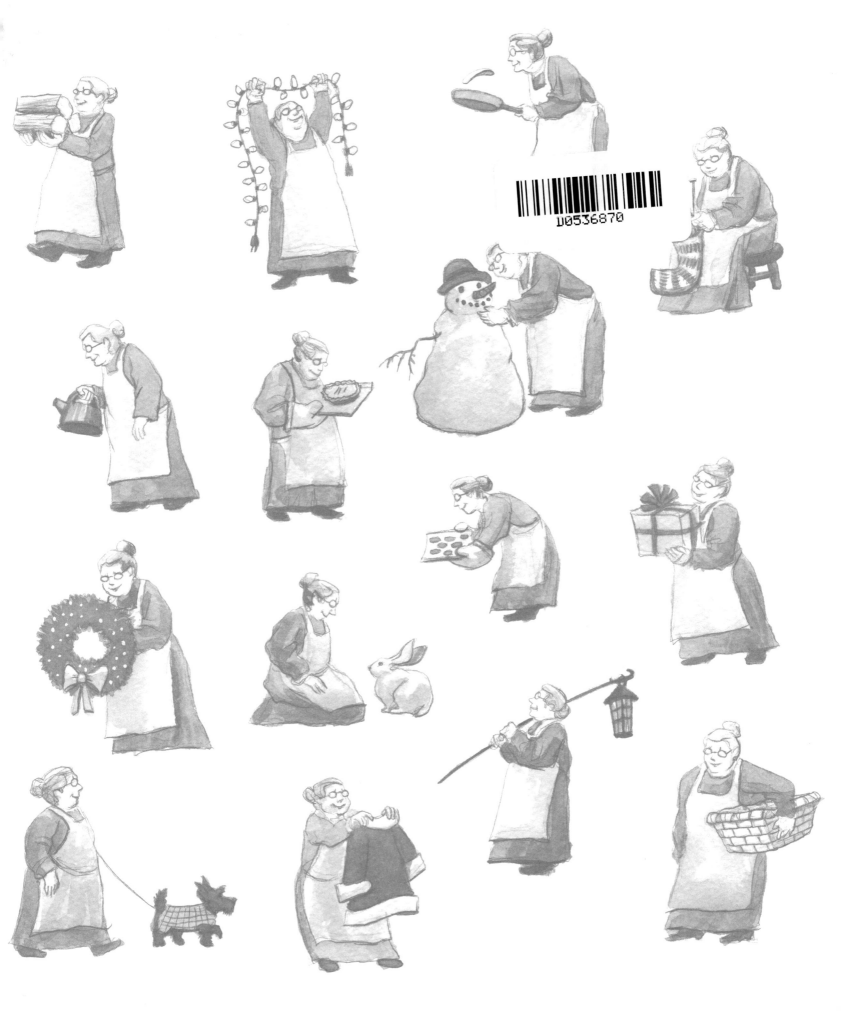

What Does Mrs. Claus Do?

by KATE WHARTON

Illustrations by CHRISTIAN SLADE

TRICYCLE PRESS
Berkeley / Toronto

*To Greg, Meredith, and Jack, for helping me
do what I do.* —K.W.

For Katherine and Nathaniel. —C.S.

Tricycle Press
an imprint of Ten Speed Press
PO Box 7123
Berkeley, California 94707
www.tricyclepress.com

Design by Betsy Stromberg
Typeset in Minister
The illustrations in this book were rendered using Winsor & Newton water-
colors and gouache, ink, graphite, and colored pencils on Strathmore cold
press 140 lb. watercolor paper.

Library of Congress Cataloging-in-Publication Data

Wharton, Kate, 1969–
  What Does Mrs. Claus Do? / by Kate Wharton ; illustrations by Christian
Slade.
     p. cm.
  Summary: Considers the many things Mrs. Claus might do while Santa
delivers toys on Christmas.
  ISBN-13: 978-1-58246-164-9 (hardcover)
  ISBN-10: 1-58246-164-3 (hardcover)
  1. Santa Claus—Juvenile fiction. [1. Stories in rhyme. 2. Santa Claus—
Fiction.] I. Slade, Christian, ill. II. Title.

PZ8.3.W55Wh 2008
[E]—dc22

                              2007046361

First Tricycle Press printing, 2008
Printed in China

1 2 3 4 5 6 — 12 11 10 09 08

E veryone knows that on Christmas Eve night,
Santa takes off on his magical flight.
But what about Mrs. Claus, not in the sleigh?
What does she do when her Santa's away?

Maybe she stays home, cleaning the mess,
reading a story, and playing some chess,
filling the stockings, and knitting some socks.
Maybe she sits by the fire and rocks.

Or maybe that's not what she does, not at all.
Perhaps Mrs. Claus hosts the Jingle Bell Ball.
The neighbors all come for the black-tie affair.
The off-duty reindeer and elves are all there.

She welcomes her guests: "I'm glad you're all here.
Tonight we are honoring veteran deer!"
The imported penguins skate by with their trays.
Ice sculptures, milk fountains, cookie buffets!

The Nutcracker Band begins rappa-tap-tapping.
They toss around tinsel and ribbon and wrapping.
Now wait just a minute. Of course she has fun,
but Christmas is work, and there's more to be done.

Perhaps Mrs. Claus runs and advises
the whole operation of Claus Enterprises.
She meets with the elves and she gives
her projections for upcoming toys
and new safety inspections.

She processes all the consumer requests.
"Perfect! Now show me the factory tests!"

She develops new products with elf engineers:
broccoli candy canes, self-cleaning deer,
supersized stockings and buccaneer bears,
paddleball rockets and rabbity chairs.
After all, Santa's job gives him so much to do,
it's best to leave details to, well…You Know Who!

Or maybe when Santa is just out of range,
she steals away for a very quick change.
On turbocharged reindeer, with elves all in black,
Mrs. Santa Claus shadows him, watching his back.

She catches the toys
that fall from the sleigh.
She keeps all the dogs
and children away,
extinguishes fires,
and switches the tags,
crumbles the cookies,
and straightens the swags.

When Santa comes home and hangs up his pack,

Mrs. Claus has just secretly beaten him back.

Are you thinking, "She can't do that all in one night!

There's not enough time!"? And perhaps you are right.

But then, if the stories of Santa are true,

why couldn't Mrs. Claus do it all too?

Whale rider, sushi chef, snowmobile chopper,
heli-ski-bungee-jump-mountaintop hopper,
Iditarod musher, movie director,
gingerbread architect, snowman inspector!

Minister, quarterback, pediatrician,
comic book artist, and master magician,
toy archeologist, mystery novelist,
nature photographer, polar geographer!

Meteorologist,
reindeer biologist,
hula instructor,
and music conductor,
acrobat, diplomat,
fashion designer,
spelunker, hoop-dunker,
candy cane miner,
offering counseling help
for the fabled,
training the reindeer
to serve the disabled.

She pilots a jet pack or hot air balloon,
works planting Christmas-tree farms on the moon!
WHAT IN THE WORLD THEN DOES MRS. CLAUS DO?
There's one thing for sure that we know to be true.

Whatever she does when her Santa's away,
she's happy to see him return in his sleigh.
She tells him, "I love you and all that you do.
And I love that I get to spend Christmas with you."